Stuff
Chicks
Like

T0364085

ISBN 978-0-7624-4415-1

Published by Running Press Book Publishers,
An Imprint of Perseus Books, LLC,
A Subsidiary of Hachette Book Group, Inc.
2300 Chestnut Street
Philadelphia, PA 19103-4371

Visit us on the web!
www.runningpress.com

Introduction

Sure, they're cute and fluffy, but
there's more to these chicks than meets
the eye. Fun-loving and adventurous,
these chicks have their own unexpected
interests and hobbies that make them
unique. On the following pages
you'll get a glimpse into the inner lives
of these lovable puffballs, enjoying
a wide range of activities, from skydiving
to hat shopping to shaking their
tail feather!

Brian likes playing jazz.

Amy likes
singing in the rain.

Kevin likes
pretending to be
a pirate.

Janet likes watching chick flicks.

Michael likes exploring.

Terri likes going to museums.

Andy likes wearing
his sunglasses
at night.

Kathy likes shaking her tail feather.

Alex likes
sunbathing.

Sue likes gardening.

Jeff likes lifting weights.

Lisa likes shopping for hats.

George likes
skydiving.

Bonnie likes counting stars.

This book has been bound
using handcraft methods and Smyth-
sewn to ensure durability.

Designed by Jason Kayser.

Edited by Jennifer Leczkowski.

The text was set in Avenir.